To my parents, Rev. Glenn and Betty Keenan, who opened their home and hearts to hundreds of precious children and became their family.
C. Hope Flinchbaugh

Published by Familius LLC, www.familius.com
PO Box 1249, Reedley, CA 93654

Familius books are available at special discounts for bulk purchases, whether for sales promotions or for family or corporate use. For more information, contact Familius Sales at orders@familius.com.

Library of Congress Control Number: 2022951298

Print ISBN 9781641709934
Ebook ISBN 9781641709064
KF 9781641709071
FE 9781641709088

Printed in China

Edited by Lindsay Sandberg
Cover design by Laurel Aylesworth
Book design by Brooke Jorden

10 9 8 7 6 5 4 3 2 1

First Edition

My House, My Family

Sometimes I live with Mommy . . .

Sometimes I stay with Dad.

But we are all a family
Whatever house I'm at.

I'm special—I'm adopted!
I love my family.

I like to catch the Tickle Monster—
Then I set him free!

My family's my mother.
Our house is way up high.
At night, we see the
stoplight change
And hear the cars whiz by.

My house is with
my Grandma.

She works and
plays with me.

It's fun when all the
cousins come—
We're quite a family!

My house is in the country,
And we need lots of room.

My family has
piles of pets
And twins are
coming soon!

I'm living at a new house.
I'm staying with new friends.
Although I love my family . . .

It's here that I fit in.

My house is really changing.
We're squeezing in somehow.

New sisters came,
and brothers too.
My family's growing—wow!

My house is made of reeds,
And we don't drive a car.
"A missionary family,"
Dad says that's what we are.

My house has ramps and railings.
See what my dog can do?

She likes to hide behind the door,
Then turns the lights off!

BOO!

I'm told my house is noisy,
Vibrations shake my hand.
Since I can't hear, my family
Makes signs I understand.

I like to live at my house;
I know I'm wanted there.
We start each day with breakfast
And we end each day
with prayer.

Sometimes I say
"I love you!"
They say, "I
love you too!"

We like to be together . . .

And do what
families do.

Discussion Questions

1. A family may have two people or ten people living in one house. How many people are in your house?

2. Families like to do different things together. What is the best thing that you like to do with your family?

3. Each family looks different. Each house looks different. Which page in this book looks a little bit like your house or your family?

4. What is the best thing about being a family?

5. Can you find the bird on each page? How many birds are there in the whole book?